ALL ABOUT ME TOO

Name	Nelly
Age	Six-ish
Time I Get Up	morning (mainly)
Bedtime	as late as possible
Max. speed (walking)	My mommy says I never walk anywear
(running)	50,000,000,000 1/2 mph
School	Not if I can help it
Likes	soccer, woodworking, welding, fixing things, fast food, Slimey the snail
Dislikes	School, people who ~~say~~ they don't like children's TV when they ~~do~~ having my hair ~~combed~~, carrots
Running away fund	50 cents
Best moment	Sticking Lil's hat down the ~~toilet~~ lavatory
Ambitions	to be a weight lifter or a rock star or a truck driver

For Rosie and Beth

Library of Congress Cataloging-in-Publication Data
Wallace, John, date.
The twins / John Wallace.
p. cm.
Summary: Twins Lil and Nelly,
who are total opposites in their likes and dislikes,
get a surprise when Nelly secretly makes some additions
to Lil's school writing project.
ISBN 0-307-10211-4 (alk. paper)
[1. Twins—Fiction. 2. Sisters—Fiction. 3. Identity—Fiction.] I. Title.
PZ7.W1567 Tw 2001 [E]—dc21 00-056164

The illustrations for this book were created with pen and watercolor.

The Twins

John Wallace

A Golden Book | New York

Golden Books Publishing Company, Inc., New York, New York 10106

Lil and Nelly were coming home from school.
Their class had been given a project and there
was a prize for the best one.

"I'm going to write all about me," said Lil.

"Well, I'm going to play outside," said Nelly.

Tap, tap, tap, tappety-tap! Lil started to type
up her project.

She worked so hard
that she had finished
by dinnertime.

Nelly decided to take a look at what Lil had written.

"There's not enough about me in here," she thought.

Nelly sat down and started to add to her sister's project.

ALL ABOUT ME
by Lil

I like to get up early.

I like to eat healthy food.

I like educational programs.

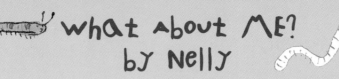

what about ME?
by Nelly

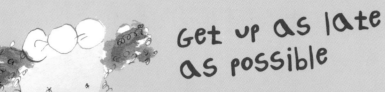

Get up as late
as possible

cake for breakfast

i like the lions that are on TV

My favorite thing is my cleaning kit.

My pet rabbit
is named Fluffy.

My hair is smooth
and blonde.

I love my shovel

My pet is
Slimey the Snail

My mom
says my hair
looks like a
haystack

THINGS I LIKE

school

the color pink

classical music

dressing up

vacuuming

and dusting

THINGS I DON'T LIKE

people who eat with their fingers

bad smells

dirt

fatty foods

loud noises

people who splash
and make a mess

THINGS I DON'T LIKE

soap

going to bed early

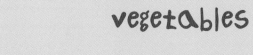

having my hair combed

vegetables

polishing my shoes

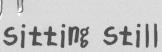

sitting still

When I grow up...

I want to be a teacher

or an airline attendant

or a princess.

well, I want
to be a
weight lifter

or a rock star

or a truck driver

Nelly was just putting
the project back where she
had found it, when Lil
walked in.

"Nelly, what are you
doing?" asked Lil.

"Oh!" said Nelly.
"I was just reading your
project. It's great!"

"Have you done yours yet?" Lil asked later.
"Oh, yes," said Nelly, with a smile.

That night, Lil dreamed she had won the prize
for the best project.

Nelly dreamed that Slimey the Snail had eaten
Lil's project for breakfast.

The next morning, Lil saw what Nelly had done.

She didn't speak to Nelly the whole way to school.

The class sat quietly while the teacher
marked the projects.

Finally, the teacher announced,
"The prize for the best project
goes to Lil *and* Nelly."

The twins couldn't believe it.

"By the way, whose idea was it to do the project together?" asked the teacher.

"Both of us had the idea *together*," said Nelly triumphantly.

"Oh, yes," Lil had to agree. "We always do everything together!"

Mine Mine

JFIC   Wallace, John.
WAL
            The twins.

$9.95

DATE			
APR 1 1 2003	3		
APR 2 8 2003			
DEC 0 7 2007			
JUN 0 2 2010			
JUN 0 2 2011			

BAKER & TAYLOR

Name	Lil
Age	five years, eleven months, and four days
Time I Get Up	6:15 a.m.
Bedtime	Monday–Friday and Sunday: 8:25 p.m. Saturday: after the nine o'clock news
Maximum Speed (walking) (running)	one mile per hour ~~I never~~ run *much slower than my sister*
~~Education~~ *School*	kindergarten
Likes	the color pink, educational programs, vacuuming and dusting, wearing sensible shoes, carrots and other healthy foods, neat and tidy things
Dislikes	silly people, children's television, rough games like playing pirates, burgers and other fatty foods, my computer breaking down
~~Savings~~ *cash*	I have $21.45 in my bank account
Best moment	learning how to use my computer
Ambitions	to become a teacher, an airline attendant, or a princess